For my parents

The story has been adapted from
Washington Irving's *Legend of Prince Ahmed Al Kamel* or *The Pilgrim of Love*,
first published in *Alhambra: a Series of Tales and Sketches
of the Moors and Spaniards* (1832).

Prince of the Birds copyright © Frances Lincoln Limited 2005
Text and illustrations copyright © Amanda Hall 2005
Hand-lettering by Andrew van der Merwe

First published in Great Britain in 2005 by
Frances Lincoln Children's Books, 4 Torriano Mews, Torriano Avenue, London NW5 2RZ
www.franceslincoln.com

Distributed in the USA by Publishers Group West

British Library Cataloguing in Publication Data available on request

ISBN 1-84507-102-6
Set in Berkeley

Printed in China
1 3 5 7 9 8 6 4 2

Prince of the Birds

AMANDA HALL

FRANCES LINCOLN CHILDREN'S BOOKS

There once lived in southern Spain, in the city of Granada, a king and queen who had one child, a boy named Ahmed. When Ahmed was born, the royal astrologers declared, "His stars are favourable, but for one – the star of love." So the worried king decided to lock his son away in a high tower, safe from the perils of love. An aged guardian taught Ahmed his lessons, but made no mention of the mysteries of the heart.

Ahmed gazed longingly out of the tiny window. His only companions were the birds on the roof above, and listening to their chatter, he began to learn their language.

Years passed. One spring morning, Ahmed was awoken by joyful birdsong. Again and again he heard the word "love", and the sound stirred his heart.

He called to a fierce hawk, "What is this love of which they sing?" But the hawk cried, "I am a warrior and know nothing of love."

Next, Ahmed asked a watchful owl returning to his roost. But the owl hooted, "I am a scholar and know nothing of love."

Then a swallow darted by, and replied to Ahmed's question, "I am a free spirit and know nothing of love."

One day, a little injured dove tumbled in through
the window. As Ahmed tended the dove back to health,
she answered his question.

"Love," she said, "is a feeling that draws two hearts together
in joy, making it misery to be apart. Prince, I have met your twin soul.
In a distant land, in another high tower, lives a fair princess who
has asked me the very same question."

Tears sprang to Ahmed's eyes, for he knew that when he met
this maiden, his soul would find peace. Sitting down, he wrote
to the princess.

 ext morning, the dove flew off with Ahmed's letter in her beak. The following weeks were a torture, as Ahmed waited for her reply. Then one evening, the dove fluttered through the window and dropped at Ahmed's feet. A hunter's stray arrow had pierced her breast.

As Ahmed clasped the little bird, he saw that she was ringed with pearls, from which hung a portrait of a beautiful young woman – his princess! But how was he to find her?

That night Ahmed, securing
one end of his turban to a hook,
climbed out into the darkness and down
to the forest below.

The watchful owl glided down too,
and Ahmed told him of his quest.

"In Seville," said the owl, "lives
a travelling parrot. He will know where
to find your princess."

In neighbouring Seville, the talking parrot was entertaining a crowd with his sparkling wit. When he heard of Ahmed's plight, he laughed. "Why seek only one love? Be like me. I am loved by the whole world."

Ahmed held the portrait under the parrot's beady eye.

"Bless me!" chortled the parrot. "It is Princess Aldegonda of the Kingdom of the Mountains! Astrologers said that the star of love threatened to throw her life into confusion. So her father has locked her away in a tower until her seventeenth birthday, when he will give her hand in marriage."

The parrot then agreed to join their search.

 Over the Sierra Morena they journeyed, until in the distance
they saw Toledo and the palace of the Kingdom of the Mountains.
The parrot flew on to the tallest tower, where Princess Aldegonda
stood, her eyes full of tears. She was gazing down at Ahmed's letter.

"Dry your tears, Princess," said the parrot, "for your beloved
awaits you outside."

The princess's eyes sparkled. "Fly, dear messenger, and tell your master
that he must prove his love by force of arms. Tomorrow a contest
will take place between my suitors."

When the parrot returned with this message, Ahmed was overjoyed –
and downcast. Aldegonda returned his love! But how was he,
a poetic young man, to win her by force of arms?

Just then, the owl said, "Within these mountains lies a secret cave,
where once lived a magician. There we shall find our solution."
And he led them to a hidden doorway.

Inside, an eerie light glinted on a golden suit of armour and weapons.
Beside them stood an enchanted horse, perfectly still as if carved from stone.
But when Ahmed touched its mane, the horse neighed and pawed the ground!

he day of the contest dawned. All eyes rested on the princess, as her eyes searched for her prince. Suddenly Ahmed, Prince of Granada, rode into view on his magic horse.

The tournament began. One suitor charged towards Ahmed. But Ahmed's horse had the strength of ten demons, and his enchanted lance flicked the brute high into the air. Inside his magic armour, Ahmed sat powerless as his horse charged headlong, unseating all his rivals.

The king, angered by this stranger, now rode in to deal with him. Alas, he met with a similar fate as the suitors, and his crown went rolling in the mud!

At sunset, Ahmed's steed turned and galloped back to the mountains.

And what of the princess? Surrounded by physicians, she would not eat or drink. The king proclaimed that whoever cured her would receive a rich reward.

Hearing this, the owl thought of a plan. He remembered that in the palace vaults, in a dusty chest, lay a magical rug. He now sent Ahmed, disguised as a physician, to the palace.

Inside the princess's chamber, the prince began to sing words from his love-letter. At once, colour returned to the princess's cheeks and she asked for a bowl of peaches. The king, overjoyed, invited the singing physician to choose his reward, and Ahmed asked for the ancient chest.

The king was surprised, but commanded the box to be brought out.

ifting the lid of the chest, Ahmed drew out the magical rug. "Such a beautiful carpet belongs at the feet of beauty," he said, and spread it before the princess. Seating himself on it, he went on, "Who can prevent what is written in the stars? For your daughter and I are twin souls, destined to love each other from birth."

At these words the carpet rose up, bearing the prince and princess off through the open door. The king and his physicians stared open-mouthed. Soon the lovers were no more than a speck in the blue heavens.